JOSEPH
and the Amazing Technicolor®
DREAMCOAT

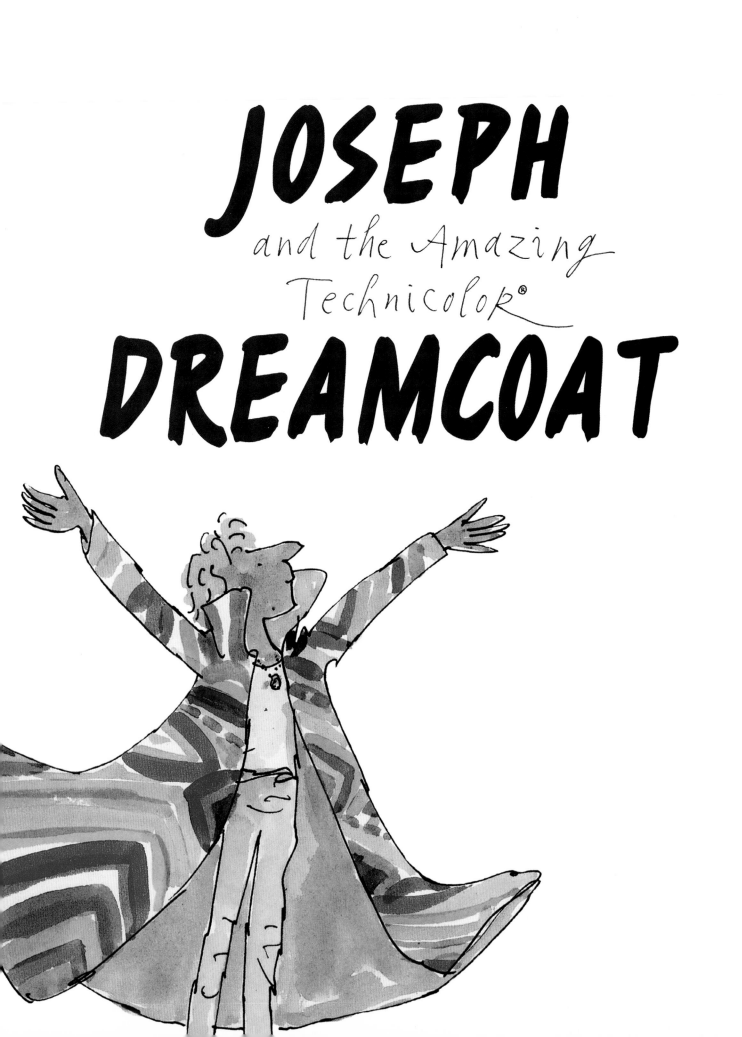

Tim Rice & Andrew Lloyd Webber

JOSEPH
and the Amazing
Technicolor®
DREAMCOAT

with
pictures by
Quentin Blake

PAVILION
CHILDREN'S

First published in Great Britain in 1982 by
Pavilion Children's Books
a division of Anova Books Ltd, 10 Southcombe Street,
London W14 0RA
www.anovabooks.com

This revised edition first published in 2012
Lyrics by Tim Rice, music by Andrew Lloyd Webber

The libretto of the musical work JOSEPH AND THE AMAZING
TECHNICOLOR® DREAMCOAT is reproduced by permission
of The Really Useful Group Ltd.

'Technicolor®' is the registered trademark of Technicolor® Inc.

Lyrics copyright © 1969, 1974, 1991 and 2012 The Really Useful
Group Ltd.

For permission to perform JOSEPH AND THE AMAZING
TECHNICOLOR® DREAMCOAT, please apply to The Really
Useful Group Ltd. www.stageamusical.com

10 9 8 7 6 5 4 3 2 1

ISBN   978-1-84365-103-1

Printed in China

Some folks dream of the wonders they'll do
Before their time on this planet is through
Some just don't have anything planned
They hide their hopes and their heads in the sand
Now I don't say who is wrong, who is right
But if by chance you are here for the night
Then all I need is an hour or two
To tell the tale of a dreamer like you

We all dream a lot – some are lucky, some are not
But if you think it, want it, dream it, then it's real
You are what you feel

But all that I say can be told another way
In the story of a boy whose dream came true
And he could be you

Way way back many centuries ago, not long after the Bible began
Jacob lived in the land of Canaan, a fine example of a family man

Jacob, Jacob and Sons, depended on farming to earn their keep
Jacob, Jacob and Sons, spent all of the days in the fields with sheep

Jacob was the founder of a whole new nation, thanks to the number of children he'd had
He was also known as Israel but most of the time his sons and wives used to call him dad

Jacob, Jacob and Sons, men of the soil of the sheaf and crook
Jacob, Jacob and Sons, a remarkable family in anyone's book

Reuben was the eldest of the children of Israel
With Simeon and Levi the next in line
Napthali and Isaachar with Asher and Dan
Zebulun and Gad took the total to nine
Benjamin and Judah, which leaves only one:
Joseph, Jacob's favourite son

Joseph's mother, she was Jacob's favourite wife
He never really loved another all his life
And Joseph was his joy because he reminded him of her

Through young Joseph Jacob lived his youth again
Loved him, praised him, gave him all he could but then
It made the rest feel second best, and even if they were
Being told 'you're also-rans' did not make them Joseph fans

BROTHERS

But where we have really missed the boat is
We're great guys but no-one seems to notice

Joseph's charm and winning smiles failed to slay them in the aisles
And their father couldn't see the danger
He could not imagine any danger
He just saw in Joseph all his dreams come true

Jacob wanted to show the world he loved his son
To make it clear that Joseph was the special one
So Jacob bought his son a coat
A multi-coloured coat to wear

Joseph's coat was elegant, the cut was fine
The tasteful style was the ultimate in good design
And this is why it caught the eye
A king would stop and stare

And when Joseph tried it on he knew his sheepskin days were gone
Such a dazzling coat of many colours, how he loved his coat of many colours
In a class above the rest, it even went well with his vest
Such a stunning coat of many colours
How he loved his coat of many colours
It was red and yellow and green and brown and blue

Joseph's brothers weren't too pleased with what they saw

BROTHERS
We had never liked him all that much before
And now this coat, has got our goat
We feel life is unfair

And when Joseph graced the scene
His brothers turned a shade of green
His astounding clothing took the biscuit
Quite the smoothest person in the district

He looked handsome, he looked smart
He was a walking work of art
Such a dazzling coat of many colours
How he loved his coat of many colours

It was red and yellow and green and brown
And scarlet and black and ochre and peach
And ruby and olive and violet and fawn
And lilac and gold and chocolate and mauve
And cream and crimson and silver and rose
And azure and lemon and russet and grey
And purple and white and pink
        and orange and blue!

To Joseph
From Dad

Joseph's coat annoyed his brothers
But what made them mad
Were the things that Joseph told them of
        the dreams he'd often had

JOSEPH

I dreamed that in the fields one day, the corn gave me a sign
Your eleven sheaves of corn all turned and bowed to mine
My sheaf was quite a sight to see, a golden sheaf and tall
Yours were green and second-rate and really rather small

BROTHERS

This was not the kind of thing we brothers like to hear
It seems to us that Joseph and his dreams should disappear

JOSEPH

I dreamed I saw eleven stars, the sun and moon and sky
Bowing down before my star, it made me wonder why
Could it be that I was born for higher things than you?
A post in someone's government, a ministry or two?

BROTHERS

These dreams of our dear brother are the decade's biggest yawn
His talk of stars and golden sheaves is just a load of corn
Not only is he tactless but he's also rather dim
For there's eleven of us and there's only one of him

The dreams of course will not come true
That is, we think they won't come true
That is, we hope they won't come true
What if he's right all along?

The dreams were more than crystal clear, the writing on the wall
Meant that Joseph some day soon would rise above them all
The accuracy of the dreams the brothers did not know
But one thing they were sure about –
The dreamer had to go

Next day, far from home, the brothers planned the repulsive crime

BROTHERS
Let us grab him now, do him in, while we've got the time

This they did and made the most of it
Tore his coat and flung him in a pit

BROTHERS
Let us leave him here all alone
And he's bound to die

When some Ishmaelites, a hairy crew, came riding by
In a flash the brothers changed their plan

BROTHERS
We need cash, let's sell him if we can
Could you use a slave, you hairy bunch of Ishmaelites?
Young, strong, well-behaved, going cheap and he reads and writes

In a trice the dirty deal was done
Silver coins for Jacob's favourite son
Then the Ishmaelites galloped off with a slave in tow
Off to Egypt where Joseph was not keen to go
It wouldn't be a picnic he could tell

JOSEPH
And I don't speak Egyptian very well

Joseph's brothers tore his precious multi-coloured coat
Having ripped it up, they next attacked a passing goat
Soon the wretched creature was no more
They dipped his coat in blood and guts and gore

Oh now brothers, how low can you stoop?
You make a sordid group, hey, how low can you stoop?
Poor, poor Joseph, sold to be a slave
Situation's grave, hey, sold to be a slave

BROTHERS

Father we've something to tell you
A story of our time
A tragic but inspiring tale
Of manhood in its prime
You know you had a dozen sons
Well now that's not quite true
But feel no sorrow, do not grieve
He would not want you to

Joseph died as he wished to
He answered duty's call
He single handed fought the beast
That would have killed us all
His blood-stained coat is tribute to his final sacrifice
His body may be passed its peak, but his soul's in Paradise

When we think of his last great battle a lump comes to our throat
It takes a man who knows no fear to wrestle with a goat
Carve his name with pride and courage
Let no tear be shed
If he had not laid down his life
We all would now be dead

There's one more angel in heaven
There's one more star in the sky
Joseph, we'll never forget you
It's tough but we're gonna get by
There's one less place at our table
There's one more tear in my eye
But Joseph, the things that you stood for
Like truth and light never die
Like love and peace never die
Like democracy never die

Joseph was taken to Egypt in chains and sold
Where he was bought by a captain named Potiphar –
Potiphar had very few cares
He was one of Egypt's millionaires
Having made a fortune buying shares in pyramids
Potiphar had made a huge pile

Owned a large percentage of the Nile
Meant that he could really live in style, and he did
Joseph was an unimportant slave who found he liked his master
Consequently worked much harder, even with devotion
Potiphar could see that Joseph was a cut above the average
Made him leader of his household, maximum promotion

Potiphar was cool and so fine
But his wife would never toe the line
It's all there in chapter thirty-nine of Genesis
She was beautiful but evil
Saw a lot of men against his will
He would have to tell her that she still was his

Joseph's looks and handsome figure had attracted her attention
Every morning she would beckon, 'Come and lie with me, love'

Joseph wanted to resist her, till one day she proved too eager
Joseph cried in vain:

JOSEPH
Please stop! I don't believe in free love!

Potiphar was counting shekels
In his den below the bedroom
When he heard a mighty rumpus
Clattering above him

Suddenly he knew his riches
Couldn't buy him what he wanted
Gold would never make him happy
If she didn't love him

Letting out a mighty roar
Potiphar burst through the door

POTIPHAR

Joseph I'll see you rot in jail,
The things you have done are beyond the pale

Poor poor Joseph, locked up in a cell
Things aren't going well, hey, locked up in a cell

JOSEPH

Close every door to me, hide all the world from me
Bar all the windows and shut out the light
Do what you want with me, hate me and laugh at me
Darken my daytime and torture my night
If my life were important I would ask will I live or die
But I know the answers lie far from this world
Close every door to me, keep those I love from me
Children of Israel are never alone
For I know I shall find my own piece of mind
For I have been promised a land of my own
Just give me a number instead of my name
Forget all about me and let me decay
I do not matter, I'm only one person
Destroy me completely, then throw me away
If my life were important I would ask will I live or die
But I know the answers lie far from this world
Close every door to me, keep those I love from me
Children of Israel are never alone
For we know we shall find our own piece of mind
For we have been promised a land of our own

Joseph's luck was really out, his spirit and his fortune low
Alone he sat, alone he thought of happy times he used to know
The prison walls were wet and black, his chains were heavy, weighed him down
A candle was his only light, the hungry rats the only sound

Go, go, go Joseph you know what they say
Hang on now Joseph, you'll make it some day
Don't give up Joseph, fight till you drop
We've read the book and you come out on top

Now into Joseph's prison cell were flung two very frightened men
Neither thought that they would ever see the light of day again

Both men were servants of Pharaoh the king
Both in the dog house for doing their thing
One was a baker, a cook in his prime
One was a butler, the Jeeves of his time

BUTLER AND BAKER
Hey Joseph! Help us if you can,
we've had dreams that we don't understand

JOSEPH
Tell me of your dreams, my friends
And I will tell you what they show
Though I cannot guarantee to get it right
I'll have a go

First the butler, trembling, took the floor
Nervously he spoke of what he saw

BUTLER
There I was standing in front of a vine
I picked me some grapes and I crushed them to wine
I gave them to Pharaoh who drank from my cup
I tried to interpret but I had to give up

JOSEPH
You will soon be free my friend
So do not worry anymore
The King will let you out of here
You'll buttle as you did before

Next the baker rose to tell his dream
Hoping it would have a similar theme

BAKER
There I was standing with baskets of bread
High in the sky I saw birds overhead
Who flew to the baskets and ate ev'ry slice
Give me the message — like his would be nice

JOSEPH
Sad to say your dream is not the kind of dream I'd like to get
Pharaoh has it in for you, your execution date is set
Don't rely on all I said I saw
It's just that I have not been wrong before

Go, go, go Joseph you know what they say
Hang on now Joseph, you'll make it some day
Sha la la Joseph, you're doing fine
You and your dreamcoat, ahead of your time!

Pharaoh he was a powerful man
With the ancient world in the palm of his hand
To all intents and purposes he was Egypt with a capital E
Whatever he did he was showered with praise
If he cracked a joke then you chortled for days
No-one had rights or a vote but the king
In fact you might say he was fairly right-wing

When Pharaoh's around then you get down on the ground
If you ever find yourself near Rameses, get down on your knees

Down at the other end of the scale
Joseph is still doing time in jail
For even though he is in with the guards
A lifetime in prison seems quite on the cards
But if my analysis of the position is right
At the end of the tunnel there's a glimmer of light
For all of a sudden indescribable things
Have shattered the sleep of both peasants and kings

Strange as it seems there's been a run of crazy dreams
And a man who can interpret could go far, could become a star
Could be famous, could be a big success

Guess what? In his bed Pharaoh had an uneasy night
He had had a dream that pinned him to his sheets with fright
No-one knew the meaning of the dream
What to do? Whatever could it mean?

Then his butler said he knew of a bloke in jail
Who was hot on dreams, could explain old Pharaoh's tale
Pharaoh said –

PHARAOH
Fetch this Joseph man, I need him to help me if he can

Chained and bound, afraid, alone, Joseph stood before the throne

JOSEPH
My service to Pharaoh has begun
Tell me your problems, mighty one

PHARAOH

Well I was wandering along the banks of the river
When seven fat cows came up out of the Nile
And right behind these fine healthy animals
Came seven other cows that were skinny and vile
Well then the thin cows ate the fat cows
Which I thought would do them good
But it didn't make them fatter
Like such a monster supper should
The thin cows were as thin as they had ever, ever, been
This dream has got me baffled, hey, Joseph what does it mean?

Now you know that kings ain't stupid, but I don't have a clue
So don't be cruel Joseph, help me now I beg of you

I was standing doing nothing in a field out of town
When I saw seven beautiful ears of corn
They were ripe, they were golden but you've guessed it
Right behind them were seven other ears that were tattered and torn
Then the bad corn ate the good corn
Man, they came up from behind, yes they did
But Joseph, here's the punch-line
It's really gonna blow your mind, flip your lid
The bad corn was as bad as it had ever, ever, been
This dream has got me all shook up, treat me nice and tell me what it means

JOSEPH

Seven years of bumper crops are on their way
Years of plenty, endless wheat and tons of hay
Your farms will boom, there won't be room
To store the surplus food you grow

After that the future doesn't look so bright
Egypt's luck will change completely overnight
And famine's hand will stalk the land
With food an all-time low

Noble king there is no doubt
What your dream is all about
All these things you saw in your pyjamas
Are long-range forecast for your farmers
And I'm sure it's crossed your mind
What it is you have to find
Find a man to lead you through the famine
With a flair for economic planning
But who this man could be I just don't know

PHARAOH

Well stone the crows, this Joseph is a clever kid
Who'd have thought that fourteen cows could mean the things he said they did?
Joseph, you must help me further, I have found a job for you
You shall lead us through this crisis. You shall be my number two

Pharaoh told his guards to fetch a chisel from the local store
Whereupon he ordered them to cut the chains that Joseph wore
Joseph got a royal pardon and a host of splendid things
A chariot of gold, a cloak, a medal and some signet rings

ADORING GIRLS

Joseph! Joseph!
Pharaoh's number two!
Joseph! Joseph!
Egypt looks to you!

Seven summers on the trot were perfect just as Joseph said
Joseph saw the food was gathered ready for the years ahead
Seven years of famine followed, Egypt did not mind a bit
The first recorded rationing in history was a hit

ADORING GIRLS

Joseph how can we ever say
All that we want to about you?
We're so glad that you came our way
We would have perished without you

PHARAOH

Joseph we are the perfect team, old buddies that's you and me
I was wise to have chosen you, you'll be wise to agree
We were in a jam, would have baffled Abraham
But now we're a partnership it's just a piece of cake

ADORING GIRLS

Greatest man since Noah
Only goes to sho-ah

JOSEPH

Anyone from anywhere
Can make it if they get a lucky break

PHARAOH

Oh — I know they treat me nice any place is paradise
When I walk in the room
They tell me they need me, pretending it's burning love
But way down I feel so bad my heart is cold and sad
As silent as the tomb
What can a fool such as I do to earn their love?
It's all too much they won't let me be I must escape the wonder of me
I feel I'm acting in a play where every line I say
Foretells impending doom
I'm playing for keeps but I know I must learn my part
Learn to be king of my heart
Yeah
Yearn to be king of my heart

(spoken)

You know, someone will say one day, all the world's a stage
But my world has always been a stage
And fate has made me lonesome tonight and every night
I need to find true love or they can bring the curtain down

I won't surrender to suspicious minds; I must break the tie that binds
Break away from shallow things the lonely world of kings
A world of golden gloom
I'll follow that dream make a tender and brand new start
Then I'll be king of my heart
The King of this old wooden heart
Then I'll be king of my heart

This could be a happy ending, perfect place to stop the show
Joseph after all has got about as far as he can go
But I'm sure that Jacob and his other sons have crossed your mind
How had famine hit the family Joseph left behind?

BROTHERS

Do you remember the good years in Canaan?
The summers were endlessly gold
The fields were a patchwork of clover
The winters were never too cold
We strolled down the boulevard together
The ambience too, too divine
Now the fields are dead and bare
No joie de vivre anywhere
Et maintenant we drink a bitter wine

Those Canaan days we used to know
Where have they gone? Where did they go?
Eh bien, raise your berets to those Canaan days

Do you remember those wonderful parties?
The splendours of Canaan's cuisine
Our extravagant, elegant soirées
The gayest the Bible has seen
It's funny but since we lost Joseph
We've gone to the other extreme
No-one comes to dinner now
We'd only eat them anyhow
I even find I'm missing Joseph's dreams
It's funny but since we lost Joseph
We've gone to the other extreme
Perhaps we all misjudged the lad
Perhaps he wasn't quite that bad
And how we miss
            his entertaining dreams

So back in Canaan the future looked rough
Jacob's family were finding it tough
For the famine had caught them unprepared
They were thin, they were ill, they were getting scared

BROTHERS
It's enough to make anyone weep
We are down to our very last sheep
We will starve if we hang around here
But in Egypt there's food going spare
They've got corn, they've got meat, they've got fruit and drinks
And if we have the time we could see the Sphinx

So they finally decided to go off to Egypt to see brother Jo
So they all lay before Joseph's feet, and begged him for something to eat

Joseph found it a strain not to laugh because not a brother among them knew who he was

JOSEPH
I shall now take them all for a ride, after all they have tried fratricide

I dreamed that in the fields one day, the corn gave me a sign
Your eleven sheaves of corn all turned and bowed to mine
I dreamed I saw eleven stars, the sun and moon and sky
Bowing down before my star, and now I realise why

How do I know where you come from? You could be spies
Telling me that you are hungry, that could be lies
How do I know who you are? Why do you think I should help you?
Would you help me? Why on earth should I believe you? I've no guarantee

BROTHERS
Grovel, grovel, cringe, bow, stoop, fall
Worship, worship, beg, kneel, sponge, crawl
We are just eleven brothers, good men and true
Though we know we count for nothing, when up next to you
Honesty's our middle name
Life is slowly ebbing from us, hope's almost gone
It's getting very hard to see us from sideways on

JOSEPH

I rather like the way you're talking, astute and sincere
Suddenly your tragic story gets me right here
All this tugging at my heart strings seems quite justified
I shall give you all you came for and a lot more beside

       Joseph handed them sackloads of food
       And they grovelled with base gratitude
       Then, unseen, Joseph nipped out around the back
       And planted a cup in young Benjamin's sack
       When the brothers were ready to go
       Joseph turned to them all with a terrible stare and said

       JOSEPH

       No! No! No! No! No!
       Stop, you robbers, your little number's up!
       One of you has stolen my precious golden cup!

Joseph started searching through his brothers' sacks
Ev'ryone was nervous, no-one could relax
Who's the thief? Who's the thief?

Is it Reuben? No!

Is it Simeon? No!

Is it Napthali? No!

Is it Dan? No!

Is it Asher? No!

Is it Issachar? No!

Is it Levi? No!

Is it Zebulun? No!

Is it Gad? No!

Is it Judah? No!

Could it be, could it be,
Could it possibly be Benjamin?
Yes! Yes! Yes!

JOSEPH

Benjamin, you nasty youth
Your crime has shocked me to the core
Never in my whole career have I encountered this before
Guards! Seize him! Lock him in a cell!
Throw the keys into the Nile as well!

Each of the brothers fell to his knees

BROTHERS
Show him some mercy, O mighty one, please
He would not do this, he must have been framed
Jail us and beat us, we should be blamed

Oh no, not he —
How you can accuse him is a mystery
Save him, take me, Benjamin is straighter than the tall palm tree
I hear the steel drums sing their song
They're singing man you know you got it wrong
I hear the voice of the yellow bird
Singing in the tree, this is quite absurd.
Oh yes, it's true, Benjamin is straighter than the big bamboo
No ifs, no buts, Benjamin is honest as coconuts
Sure as the tide wash the golden sand
Benjamin is an innocent man
Sure as bananas need the sun
We are the criminal guilty ones
Oh no, not he —
How you can accuse him is a mystery
Save him, take me, Benjamin is straighter than the tall palm tree

And Joseph knew by this his brothers now were honest men
The time had come at last to reunite them all again

JOSEPH
Can't you recognise my face?
Is it hard to see
That Joseph who you thought was dead — your brother — is me?

BROTHERS
Joseph, Joseph, is it really true?
Joseph, Joseph, is it really you?

So Jacob came to Egypt
No longer feeling old
And Joseph went to meet him
In his chariot of gold

JOSEPH

I closed my eyes, drew back the curtain
To see for certain, what I thought I knew
Far, far away, someone was weeping
But the world was sleeping, any dream will do

I wore my coat, with golden lining
Bright colours shining, wonderful and new
And in the east, the dawn was breaking
And the world was waking, any dream will do

A crash of drums, a flash of light
My golden coat flew out of sight
The colours faded into darkness, I was left alone

May I return, to the beginning
The light is dimming, and the dream is too
The world and I, we are still waiting
Still hesitating, any dream will do

Give me my coloured coat, my amazing coloured coat.

Any dream will do...